Miss Dose
the Doctors' Daughter

by ALLAN AHLBERG

with pictures by
FAITH JAQUES

Puffin

Viking

PUFFIN/VIKING

Published by the Penguin Group
Penguin Books Ltd, 27 Wrights Lane, London W8 5TZ, England
Penguin Books USA Inc., 375 Hudson Street, New-York, New York 10014, USA
Penguin Books Australia Ltd, Ringwood, Victoria, Australia
Penguin Books Canada Ltd, 10 Alcorn Avenue, Toronto, Ontario, Canada M4V 3B2
Penguin Books (NZ) Ltd, 182–190 Wairau Road, Auckland 10, New Zealand

Penguin Books Ltd, Registered Offices: Harmondsworth, Middlesex, England

First published 1988
9 10

Text copyright © Allan Ahlberg, 1988
Illustrations copyright © Faith Jaques, 1988

Educational Advisory Editor: Brian Thompson

Printed and bound in Great Britain by
William Clowes Limited, Beccles and London
Filmset in Century Schoolbook (Linotron 202) by
Rowland Phototypesetting (London) Ltd

British Library Cataloguing in Publication Data
Ahlberg, Allan
  Miss Dose the doctors' daughter – (Happy families).
  I. Title   II. Jaques, Faith   III. Series
  823'.914[J]   PZ7

ISBN Paperback 0 14 03.2346 5
ISBN Hardback 0–670–81692–2

Dora Dose was a doctor's daughter.
Well, really she was
a double doctor's daughter.
Her mum was a doctor
and her dad was a doctor.
Dora liked to pretend *she* was a doctor.

Each morning, when her dad
came down to breakfast, he said,
"Is there a doctor in the house?"
And Dora shouted, "Yes – me!"
She took his temperature
and tapped his knee with
her little doctor's hammer.
She told him to say "Ah!"

Dora Dose had a pretend doctor's bag,
a pretend doctor's waiting-room
and six pretend patients.

Dora's patients were:
her little brother, her baby brother,
her teddy, two dolls,
and – sometimes – the cat.

Dora took their temperatures
and tapped their knees with
her little doctor's hammer.
She told them to say "Ah!"

But Dora was not happy
being a pretend doctor.
Her thermometer didn't really work.
Her doctor's hammer was a toy.
Her patients would not do
as they were told.

"Next please!" said Dora.
And her little brother said,
"It's *my* turn to be the doctor."
"Next please!" said Dora.
And her baby brother crawled off.

"Next please!" said Dora.
And the cat *ran* off.
"Next please!" said Dora.
And the teddy and the dolls . . .
just sat there.

"I wish I was a real doctor,"
said Dora.
And she went into the kitchen
and bandaged up her mum.
Then – one morning – this happened.
Dora Dose woke up
and went into her baby brother's room.

She was thinking of
taking his temperature.
But what did she find?
Her baby brother was awake,
smiling – and *covered in spots!*

"Oh!" said Dora.
She ran into her little brother's room.
He was covered in spots, too.

Then she ran into her parents' room,
and they were covered in spots.
"Is there a doctor in the house?"
said Mr Dose.
And Dora said, "Yes – me!"
"What we need is the spots medicine,"
said Mrs Dose.
She began to get out of bed.
"I'll go," said Dora.

Dora went downstairs
to her mum and dad's surgery.
She got the spots medicine.
She gave her dad a spoonful,
her mum a spoonful,
her little brother a spoonful
and her baby brother half a spoonful.
She also tapped her baby brother's knee
and told him to say "Ah!"

At nine o'clock Dora looked
in her mum and dad's waiting-room.
And what did she find?
Lots of patients waiting –
real patients – real *spotty* patients!

"What they need is the spots medicine,"
said Mr Dose.
He began to get out of bed.
"I'll go," said Dora.

Dora went downstairs
to the surgery again.
She put on her mum's white coat.
She picked up her dad's stethoscope.
She sat in the doctor's chair.

"Next please!" said Dora.
And the first patient came in.
"You're a little doctor," he said.
"Yes," said Dora.
She gave him a bottle of spots medicine.

"Next please!" said Dora.
And the second patient came in.
"You're a *very* little doctor," she said.
"Yes," said Dora.
She gave her *two* bottles.

"Next please!" said Dora.
And the next patient came in –
and the next – and the next –
and the next.
Most of them said
what a little doctor Dora was.
None of them said
it was *their* turn to be the doctor.

When all the patients had gone,
Dora Dose went upstairs.
She sat on her parents' bed.
She took her dad's temperature.
She told her mum to say "Ah!"
"Is there a doctor in the house?"
said Dora.
"Yes," said her dad.
And her mum said, "You!"

A few days later, the doorbell rang
at the doctors' house.
Mr Dose opened the door.
And what did he find?
It was all those patients again.
They had come to say "thank you".
Their spots had gone.
"Is there a *little* doctor in the house?"
they said.
"Well," said Mr Dose,
"there's a little *spotty* doctor."

And so there was.
Doctor Dora was up in her room,
as happy as could be.
She had a real doctor's bag,
a real thermometer,
a real hammer . . .

. . . and a perfect patient.

The End